I0608278

JAKE

UNDERCOVER LOVER SERIES – BOOK III

Cover Design by: Bella Media Management

JAKE

UNDERCOVER LOVER SERIES — BOOK III

C. A. SALO

CHAPTER 1

JAKE LET THE CLUTCH OUT and sat back enjoying the morning ride into the station. The weather was perfect. He did as he was trained, always took a different way in, until he hit this part of the highway. If he didn't take it, he wouldn't be able to get to work for almost two hours. Sighing, he turned his head when a black bike came up beside him and smiled. The rider, a female, had been flirting with him for a couple of months. He didn't know who she was; her helmet hid that fact from him. Grinning, he sat a bit straighter as she took off down the highway and hit the clutch and gas to catch up with her. She'd slow down, go behind him, speed back up. After riding side by side for several miles, she blew him an imaginary kiss, by touching her fingers to where her mouth would be under the tinted face cover of her helmet before taking off as she did every time. He knew he couldn't catch her; he tried that the first week she'd shown up. She rode a bee, or that's what he called them, a sports bike, and if you got enough of them together, they sounded like a hive.

Jake frowned, feet braced apart, arms crossed over his chest. Who in the hell did this bike belong to? It had never been parked in the garage before, at least not that he had seen. Walking around the 2017 Suzuki GW250, he knew they had to be a cop and a female at that. Every morning for the past two months, this bike and its driver would mess with him on his way into the station.

"What are you doing, shopping for a new look?" Gabe asked, as Jake strolled in.

"It's this bike, man. This is the one I've been telling you about, the one that fucks with me every morning."

Jake turned at Gabe's chuckle. "What's so funny?"

"You moron and the fact you can't figure out who rides it." Gabe slapped him on the shoulder as he took off for the stairs. "Let's go, Columbo. We've got work to do."

Jake flung one last scowl at the terrorizer before following his brother. "If you know who it is why won't you tell me?"

"You're a detective, figure it out."

~~*~~

"What in the hell is wrong with you?" Zack asked.

"That friggin' bike. I can't figure out who in the hell rides it. No one at the station will give the person up, and frankly, it's frustrating the hell out of me."

"Would that be sexual frustration?" Mitch chuckled.

"Fuck you." Jake lifted the beer to his mouth as they both chuckled. If he were honest with himself, they were speaking the truth. Her body in tight leather and she knew how to ride- it was just- sexy.

"What's he doing?" Catia asked, as she sat down with a beer.

"Daydreaming." Mitch said.

"About?"

"The female who rides that Suzuki." Zack grinned.

"Oh."

"Shut up." Jake tipped his bottle again. "How are you doing Catia?"

"Ok."

"That wound heal up all right?" Jake met her gaze.

"Ah yeah, they took the stitches out yesterday."

"Hey, you don't know who drives the Suzuki, do you?"

"Ah." Her gaze whipped to Zack when he chuckled. "Yeah, why?" she asked slowly, glancing back at Jake.

"She's driving me nutty and no one will tell me who she is. It's starting to piss me off."

"You're pissed because she's driving you nutty or no one will tell you who she is?"

"Both." Glancing down when three cell phones went off, Jake took his out. "Damn."

"Yeah, see you later Catia." Mitch said, as he rose from the table with Zack.

Jake set his bottle down and rose up, tucking the cell back into his pocket. "I'll catch you later."

"All right be safe out there." Catia said.

"Thanks." Jake headed to the door, waving at Walt on his way by, and followed Mitch and Zack to the station.

~~*~~

"Hey, what's going on with you?" Marc asked.

"Hey cuz." Jake answered as he stared out the window. "You haven't seen that Suzuki, have you?"

"Not in a few days. Why, she still playing cat and mouse with you?"

"Yeah," glancing over Jake met his gaze as Marc leaned against the wall. "Do you know who she is?"

"I have my suspicions, but anything definite, no."

Jake sighed. "My brothers know, but they won't spill."

"Why not?"

"No clue. They tell me, I'm a detective, figure it out."

"Why don't you ask Gloria? Don't they monitor the garage?"

Jake glanced to the left. "Yeah, I think you're right. Shit, it's after five. I'll have to catch her tomorrow."

Marc chuckled. "Yeah, I don't think your mojo will work with Bill."

~~*~~

Jake cruised on the highway, the temperature hotter than the last few days, glanced to the right, and stared at the bike coming up off the ramp to ride next to him. She tilted her head when he didn't smile and signed *bad day* with the hand closest to him. Jake lifted his hand and motioned, two fingers up and straight ahead of them. She leaned down, hit the gas, and took off. "Son of a bitch," he grumbled. Hitting the gas, he tried catching her, but Harleys like his were not built for speed, like that crotch rocket she was on.

Jake glared at the Suzuki as he strode by the damn thing and headed up to where the monitors were. Knocking on the door, he waited a moment before entering. "Hey, Ms. Gloria."

"Well, hey sugar, what brings you up here?"

Jake smiled. He loved Gloria. She was old enough to be his grandmother, had worked for the department over thirty years, and had been a friend of the family since she scolded his dad when he was a rookie. "Well, I kinda need a favor."

"Uh-huh. Spill."

Jake sat next to her. "There's a Suzuki in the garage. I

know you monitor the garage as well as the station. I need to know who drives it."

Gloria burst out laughing.

Jake frowned. "Why are you laughing at me?"

"Ah shug, this little girl has your insides all swirled up, huh?"

His brows arched. "You know who she is?"

Gloria cupped his cheek in her hand. "So, do you, Jakob. She's right in front of your face, hiding in plain sight."

Jake sighed as she patted his cheek. "Why does she drive me crazy?"

"Because honey, it's the mystery that's got your craw."

"What happens when I know who she is? What happens if I'm not attracted to her?"

"Well now, that's up to you. Go with your gut. Even if she's not someone you'd typically ask out, what's wrong with giving it a shot? You know, my Henry was not my type at all. That man was all glamour and running around with those seventies' leisure suits. By the good Lord, I couldn't stand that, but that man didn't give up, and he finally wore me down. Turned out to be the best thing in my life."

"Thanks Gloria." Leaning in he kissed her cheek.

"Anytime, shug."

Smiling, he stepped out, heading down to the squad room. "Hey, girl."

"Hey Jake." Catia smiled as she stepped into the elevator.

"You just coming in?"

"Yeah. Heading to briefing, you?"

"Squad room," Jake turned to meet her gaze. "Hey, the other night you said you knew who drove the Suzuki."

Her gaze waivered for a moment. "Yeah."

"Want to give her up? I mean…"

"No one will tell you, huh?"

"No, they tell me she's right in front of my face, I'm a Detective, figure it out."

"Even your brothers?"

"Especially them," he frowned. "They think this is funny as hell."

"Huh."

"I mean, we're friends, right you know, you and I worked close on the case with Tam and I thought, why not ask you. You're a girl and…"

"Glad you noticed."

Jake stared as the door opened and she stepped out, turned and looked back at him.

"What if you don't like her, like that?"

"How the hell am I supposed to know if I don't get a shot to get to know her off the job?"

"What if she's afraid of being rejected?"

Jake started laughing. "Seriously?" He rushed the last word as the door closed. "Damn!"

~~*~~

"Hey, do you have Catia's number?" he asked striding up to Zack and Gabe.

"Not on hand, why?" Zack asked.

"Because she knows who rides the demon bike and didn't have time to tell me before she got off the elevator."

"Does she now." Gabe grinned.

"Yeah. I hate to bother her before she goes on shift, but she may be able to call me when she has a break."

"Why don't you go ask the desk sergeant. I'm sure she'd help you out."

Jake snorted. "Yeah, right. Matilda would call in a favor from me if I asked her anything." Shaking his head, he picked up a file. "Forget it, I'll get her later, what do we have going on with this?"

CHAPTER 2

CATIA FROWNED. HE LAUGHED. THAT ass actually laughed at her. She tapped the pencil against the table. She was a good cop, and hard when she had the badge on, but what the hell would make him think, any woman wouldn't have confidence issues? Especially if she hadn't revealed to him who she was yet. Seriously, she was a rough tough flaky puff, rough on the outside and creamy with a bit of flakiness. She was such a big softy, she didn't even know how she did her job, or maybe that was why. "Shit."

"You all right?" Parker asked as they headed out to the patrol car.

"Yeah, just something personal."

"You know, I heard Jake Mac Cloud was hanging around your bike."

Catia rolled her eyes. "Yes, I know."

"Are you going to tell him? You're the one messing with him every day."

"That's what I'm contemplating."

Parker chuckled. "Shit, girl, go for it. If I wasn't married and twenty years younger, I'd probably hit on him. The Mac Cloud boys take after their daddy: strong, hot and all man."

Catia smiled over at Parker. She'd been on the force for

fifteen years, liked patrol and stayed there. Catia admired her skill, logic and hardworking ethics. You didn't see that much anymore. Most people were always angling to move up, but Parker was happy where she was, on the street. "Noted."

~~*~~

Catia sighed as she grabbed her helmet out of her locker. What a freaking day. Busy and out of control. It was as if every person they ran across had something against cops and wanted nothing more than to argue with them. Parker did her uniform justice. She didn't put up with that and set them straight in her polite, but firm, "now honey, this is what we have to do" mode. Stretching her neck, she came around the corner, stopped short and backed up quickly. Her back hit the wall and her chest rose, nipples brushing against her bra. Jake was sitting on her bike. Shit, shit, shit!

Two choices: fight or flight. Grabbing the door, she headed back to the locker room, tossed her helmet in her locker, and headed to the front of the station. Frack, why was she such a wimp when it came to Jake? Sitting down, Catia took her cell out and googled a cab company. She was about to hit the call button when a Harley Fat Boy stopped in front of her. Her gaze met Jake's. "Ah, hey, what's up?"

"What are you doing out here?"

"Ah, getting a cab."

"For what?"

"Ride home."

"Hop on, I'll take you."

"Oh, well, I don't want to put you out, Jake. I mean…"

"Please. I'm headed to the Fay for a beer. Hop on."

Catia's gaze followed when he reached around and lowered the pegs for her feet. "Sure. I'm over on Plumadore, Venetian Apartments."

"You want to hit the Fay first?"

"Not tonight, but I'll take a rain check." Sitting behind him, Catia drew her sunglasses down, glad she'd left her hair in a tied cub at her neck. She set her feet on the pegs, and smiled at him. "All right, hot stuff. Let's roll." She listened to his chuckle as he pulled back onto the street.

Damn, her pussy was clenching. Grabbing the back handle instead of him, she lay one hand on his back lightly. She knew by speaking with others, Jake didn't have anyone on the back often; none of the Mac Cloud's did. From what she understood, the brothers were very picky about who rode with them. They didn't just swing the latest fuck on the back and go. It could be due to their undercover status with the Special Investigations Unit; they couldn't be seen with just anyone. Then again, he let her get on and a cop on the back of a bike to an undercover, could lead to trouble if seen by the wrong element. She knew Zack had a hell of a time with Sydney when they were stopped by a suspected drug lord that the SIU and FEDs were working a case together on, while Sydney was targeted for her own case.

Catia leaned forward as Jake leaned back a bit at a stoplight.

"Do you need me to pick you up in the morning?"

Shit, she hadn't thought of that and glanced over when a red sports car stopped beside them, the chick driving, ogling Jake, winking at him. The devil made her do it. Okay, maybe her lust for him too. Leaning forward, her breasts rubbed his back, nipples hard, her lips at his ear, hand creeping around his rib cage. Oh damn, what a six pack. "That would be great."

"All right." His hand landed on her thigh.

Catia grinned leaning back a bit when the light turned green. It was a nice evening the humidity down and the wind blowing. This calm was one of the things she loved about riding: just you, the wind, and your bike beneath you. She knew he loved it too as he took the freeway they both drove every day and when he came to speed, he leaned back, placing his hand back on her thigh as they coasted down the highway.

Catia leaned forward when he turned into her apartments and pointed to the right. They were pretty nice apartments, more like a townhouse. "One-twelve." His nod let her know he heard her as he parked in the spot with her number on it, before shutting it down.

"These are pretty nice units. My cousin Samantha lived here a while back."

"I was lucky enough to get one when I moved to town. The property manager said they usually had a year wait list, but she'd gone down every single one the day I walked in and no one could take it." Getting off, she stood off to the side, took her sunglasses off, and met his gaze as he did the same." You know, I…"

"Whoa, hey Ms. Catia, is that a Harley?"

A gentle smile lined her lips. "Hey George, yes it's a Harley, and this is my friend Jake."

Catia chuckled as the ten-year-old walked around the bike. "He likes bikes."

"I can tell." Jake smiled.

"It's a Fat Boy, right?" George asked. "How does it ride? Does oil pour out of it? Can you get it any louder?"

"You're right, it's a Fat Boy." Jake said as he went down on one knee next to the boy.

Catia grinned as Jake answered his questions. He was patient and listened to George's excitement. Catia waved when his mother came out. "Hey, Jen."

"Hey Catia. George, leave Catia and her friend alone, my goodness son."

"But mom, it's a Fat Boy!"

"Yes, I'm aware it's a Harley."

"Not just any Harley, mom. A Fat boy!" His little hand ran along the leather seat.

"I'm sorry, he's…"

"He's fine." Jake smiled.

Catia tilted her head, liking how Jake picked up on George's disabilities and smiled at Jen when she turned wide eyes her way. "Hey George, I know you want to ask a ton more questions, but Jake was just dropping me off, hun."

"Oh." His little head went down a bit.

"Hey George, no worries. I can swing by on another day when I have more time." Jake said.

"Really?"

Catia's heart melted. His little smile warmed her insides. "George, ask him about his brothers."

"You have brothers?"

"I do and they all ride different Harley's." Jake smiled.

"Oh man!" Clapping his hands, he jumped up and down "Do you think they'd let me see theirs too?"

"I guarantee it."

"Oh God, Catia. What have you started?" Jen chuckled.

"I'm not sure." Catia laughed.

"Come on George, let Catia say goodbye to Jake."

"Ok. Bye, Jake." George shook his hand and then hugged Catia. "Bye, Ms. Catia."

"Bye, honey. I'll see you later." Catia hugged him to her, loving the little guy. "You be good for mom."

Catia grinned when he took off after his mother. "So how are you going to pull that off, Mac Cloud?"

"What are you doing Saturday?"

Catia tilted her head, eyes squinted as she met his gaze. "Nothing."

"Good, cookout Saturday, check with Jen. I'll get the guys here."

"Are you serious?" Catia met his gaze head on.

"Yeah."

"I can cook, but I don't have a grill or stuff for a cookout, Jake."

"No problem, just make your favorite dish. I'll handle the rest."

Catia stepped up to him as he turned to sit on his bike. "How are you going to pull that off, Mac Cloud?"

Jake chuckled. "I love it when you get flustered. You call me Mac Cloud."

"I do not."

"You do too."

Catia paused, mouth open and shut it. "All right, I guess I do."

"Just see if Jen's available Saturday. I'll take care of the rest."

"I'll text her later."

"Good. Now, why don't you come a little closer."

Head tilted, she took a slow step forward and he hooted with laughter.

"My god Andres, you act as though I'm going to eat you up."

Catia drew back and punched his bicep.

"Damn woman." He laughed.

"What the hell did you want me to move forward for anyways?"

"Maybe to kiss you."

Catia jumped back. "Ki, kiss me, but I mean, why?"

"What the hell do you mean why? You were shooting out signals on the bike, or was that because another woman was checking me out and you were on the back?"

Her chest lifted with a deep breath. "Maybe all of it."

Jake grinned. "I can work with that."

"Jake."

"I'll see you tomorrow morning, Andres. Seven thirty?"

"That's good. Oh, and expect to see a little face in the window when you start her up." Catia smiled when he winked at her before lowering his sunglasses and starting his bike up, and true to word, up popped George in a window. Catia grinned as Jake backed out, turned his head and waved back at George before he took off. She didn't think he'd be that good with children, but he turned out to be better. In a matter of minutes, Jakob Mac Cloud showed her a side that had her heart tearing down a wall. "Damn it."

~~*~~

Catia smiled, waved at Jake as they hit the main lobby of the police department, only to be stopped by Zack, who walked toward them.

"Vehicle still down, Andres?"

Her brow arched. "Ah, yeah, something like that."

She scooted off to the locker room. Damn, Zack knows. "Shit." Grabbing her uniform, she tossed it on.

Tucking a strand of hair behind her ear, she headed to the briefing, seeing Jake at the front desk talking to the Sergeant about the bike and who drives it. Her brows went up when Sergeant Matilda Jenkins, motioned for her to come over.

Jenkins grinned. "I don't know why this is so hard for you, Mac Cloud. Everyone but you has figured it out."

Catia groaned as she approached with a smile. "Yes, desk Sergeant?"

"Mac Cloud needs a uniform on a protective detail."

Catia caught keys.

"Car sixteen, I'll let briefing know."

"Yes, Ma'am." Heading out she met Jake's gaze as he stepped beside her.

"Hey, if everyone but me knows, how come no one will fill me in?" Jake asked as they headed outside.

"I don't know."

~~*~~

Oh, my, God. She was so sick of hearing about the damn bike, the demon bike, her freaking bike. She'd heard nothing about anything else but the damn bike and its rider all day, during the detail, every moment they got, and frankly it was starting to piss her off. They were in the garage, heading up to the locker rooms, and Catia stopped cold, when he started complaining about the bike again, the moment they walked by it.

She waited until he turned to look at her, hand on hip. "My God, Mac Cloud. Is that all you can talk about is the stupid bike and its driver? Yes, it's still there, see the fucking thing? You walked right by it! Why in the hell did you want a kiss from me yesterday when all you have on your damn mind is that and the female who drives it?" She pointed in the direction of the bike. "You're supposed to be a Detective, so figure it out!" Catia stormed by him and bumped his shoulder hard.

CHAPTER 3

JAKE STEPPED INTO THE STATION'S gym a day later, his gaze finding Catia as she punched a bag. She was right, he was obsessed with the damn bike and it mysterious driver. Gabe told him he was stupid and couldn't see a good thing right in front of his face. Damn she was hot, and he liked working with her, Catia proved to be intelligent as well as a good cop. To hell with this bee chick, she was probably a greenhorn straight out of the academy or a civilian working at the station who had a thing for cops.

Jake stepped out of the doorway and into the gym, smiling when she met his gaze and lowered her hands. "Hey."

"Hey."

"Want to grab a drink?"

"Sure, let me clean up."

"I'll be up in the squad room."

~~*~~

Jake met her gaze as he lifted the bottle to his lips. "Sorry about yesterday."

Catia shrugged. "It is what it is."

"Nah, I was an ass. You were right, and you called me on it."

"A man who can admit when he's an ass, impressive."

"It took me a day to figure it out, but yeah, I was an ass and I'm sorry."

Catia smiled as she lifted her beer bottle. "Accepted."

Jake clinked her bottle with his. "So, tell me, do you miss Miami?"

"No, not really."

"Why did you move?"

"My dad passed away recently. I had no reason to stay there."

Jake watched as she twirled the bottle with her fingers, her gaze on it. "No other family?"

"No. Mom passed when I was thirteen. My parents came over from Cuba, they were young. Their family told them to go, go to America and have a better life. So they did. They worked hard, and with the help of others in the community were able to learn English, About two years later, they obtained their citizenship, then I came along."

"So, you didn't leave a boyfriend behind?"

Catia chuckled as she met his gaze. "Are you one-minded, Mac Cloud?"

Jake shrugged with a grin.

"No, no boyfriends. You know how it is. If you're a cop, it's hard to find someone who can live with that, unless it's another cop. I've noticed most of the time, if they're not in law enforcement somehow, or come from a family which is, it's like, I don't know… they try to change you, think they can rework your inner self to do something else."

"Yeah, I've had a few of those."

"How is it all you boys turned out to be cops?"

"It's in the blood. For some reason, we all followed my dad. Never wanted to do anything else."

"Your dad- I've heard a little about him."

"Yeah, he was well-known at the station house. He was a good cop."

"I heard he was killed on duty."

"Yeah. I was small, eight maybe. I remember that night." Jake lifted his beer, swallowing heavily. "So, are we on for Saturday?"

"Oh, damn, yeah. I forgot to tell you. Yes, Jen said you were nuts, but yeah, cookout Saturday."

Jake grinned. He liked when her eyes lit up with excitement. "Are you working tomorrow?"

"Yes, I traded with Parker. She's taking my Saturday shift so we can do the cook out."

"Gloria Parker?"

"Yeah, that's her. she's been my partner, showing me the ropes around here."

"Gloria's awesome. If you don't know it, she'll teach you. Even if you do know it, she'll show you a better way.

"I've noticed. She has so much experience and the way she goes about it, holy crap, they need to put every rookie with her."

"Exactly." Downing his beer, he set it on the table as she did the same. "Ready?"

"Yeah."

Jake opened the door to his truck for her and shut the door. Damn, she had his cock hard. Walking around the front, he opened the door and sat down.

"What made you take the truck instead of your bike?"

"Sometimes I just get a hunkering to drive it. Why, prefer the bike?"

Catia chuckled. "No, the truck is fine. It surprised me to see you in it."

"Yeah, unless it's bad weather or something, you'll see me on the bike." Jake grabbed his cell when it went off. "Yeah?"

"You're going on with me. Where are you?" Gabe said.

"Driving Catia home. We just left the Fay."

"Meet me at the station." Gabe said.

"ETA?"

"Now."

Jake hung up and glanced over at Catia. "Damn, I'm not going to be able to bring you home. Can you find a ride from the station? I need to meet Gabe."

"Ah yeah, no problem."

"I'm sorry Catia, I'd let you drive the truck home, but I don't have my bike and I sure as hell am not riding on the back of Gabe's."

Catia chuckled. "Oh, that would be a sight. So, is this how you're getting everything to the apartment on Saturday?"

"No, Sydney is going to drive Zack's truck, he's going to load up the back with the grill. Oh, by the way, Mom's coming, if that's ok. When I asked if I could borrow her grill and picnic tables, she asked why, so she's going to haul them over."

"Of course, it's okay. My God, you're having her deliver stuff. If anything she deserves to eat the rewards for helping."

Jake turned to her with a smile. "Thanks."

"No, you tell her, thank you for helping. My gosh, I still can't believe you pulled this all together within twenty-four hours Jake."

"It just took a few calls." Jake backed up in a parking space and parked in the stations garage, turned off the engine and turned, meeting her gaze. Unbuckling his seat belt, he leaned over. Gently cupping her cheek, he met her gaze. Jake lowered his head, softly brushing his lips across hers. His thumb caressed her bottom lip, opening her mouth slowly, giving her a chance to stop at any time. When Catia tilted her head granting him better access, he took it. His fingers slid into her hair as his tongue darted in. Catia moaned and he heard the snip of her seatbelt being unclipped, then she scooted closer. Both jumped back when the garage door hinges echoed the door being opened.

"Oh- um- wow." Catia breathed.

"Yeah, sorry about that."

"About what?"

"I ask you out for a drink and ended up attacking you."

Catia chuckled. "I think the feeling is mutual, Jake. I did kiss you back."

Jake glanced over when an officer waved at them as he walked by, and lifted his hand in acknowledgement, as did Catia. "I'll call you when I get back."

"Okay. Be safe."

The corner of his mouth lifted. "You too." Leaning in, he met her halfway, no hesitation this time. Damn, he liked kissing her. Jake and Catia jumped apart as someone pounded on the hood of his truck. Jake turned his head with narrowed eyes. "Christ's sakes, Gabe!"

"Come on lover boy, we're on. Catia." He nodded to them before moving off.

"Damn ass," Jake grumbled as Catia chuckled.

"I'll let you get, before he comes back." Catia leaned in, kissing him quickly. He smiled as she opened the door and hopped out. "Take care."

Jake

Jake nodded, before he started the truck up. He needed to go get his bike. "You too Cat."

~~*~~

Jake made it to Catia's apartment by ten-thirty. Backing in, he smiled as she appeared in the rearview mirror. Damn, his dick went hard. The jean shorts she had on made her legs look a mile long. They finished the assignment early this morning and after sleeping a few hours, he was up and ready to go in more ways than one. The guys would be here in about an hour, but he wanted some time alone with Catia. Jake snorted. Right. What he really wanted to do was put her against the nearest wall and hammer his cock into her so hard they'd both be screaming. "Fuck."

"Hey you." Catia grinned.

Jake opened the door and met her gaze when she chuckled.

"What's going through your mind?"

"If you knew you'd probably run screaming."

Her tinkling laugh just made it worse.

"I don't scare that easily, Mac Cloud."

"And I should have gotten off in the shower this morning."

"I did."

Jake growled, grabbed her and yanked her between his legs, his mouth settling on hers.

Catia groaned, her hands on his thighs as she moved closer.

"How fast do those shorts come off?"

"As fast as it takes for you to put a condom on."

Jake moaned. "Damn baby, you're going to kill me." His hot breath hitting her lips, he nibbled and sucked her bottom one into his mouth. He touched his forehead to hers when he heard his name called out. "I love kids, but they seem to have this radar of the wrong timing."

Catia chuckled. "That's what they do."

Jake slid down when she backed up, kissed her quickly and then went to say hi to George.

~~*~~

Catia laughed as she helped load the grills and tables into the trucks. Several of the other kids around came over, and she liked how the Mac Cloud's offered anyone who came by something to eat. My God, their mother was amazing. She'd never seen so much food before. They gladly opened their arms and food to anyone. Zack even brought a children's waterslide that they inflated, but honestly, she couldn't wait until she was alone with Jake. She knew she shouldn't, but damn. That man did something to her. *'Yeah dumb ass, he makes you horny.'* It hadn't happened in a long time. Shutting the tail gate, she turned when cell phones started going off, to see Jake, his brothers and cousin checking them and a quiet "shit" from Jake.

"Oh, here they go. My boys are on." Beth Mac Cloud stated.

"Yeah, it's something to watch, huh?"

"It sure is."

Catia met Jake's gaze as he approached and noticed his mom moving off to the side.

"I have to go."

"I see that."

"Damn, I wanted to get some alone time with you."

Catia smiled. "Me too." Jake smiled back, and she

lifted up on her toes to meet him, lips touching softly. "Be safe."

"I'll do my best." He leaned in and Catia met him for a longer kiss. "I gotta go."

"I know." Backing up when the sound of Harley's roared, she smiled. "See you later, Mac Cloud."

Jake winked. "You can bet on it."

Catia turned as he headed to his bike his uncle Walt had shown up with, and smiled as they all waved at George as they headed out. That man. No matter what they wanted or the events and fun of the day, he had not forgotten why they had set it up. Damn, he was going to make all of her walls crumble.

~~*~~

Jake smacked Gabe as they walked down the hall of the station, heading out. "You're such a damn smart ass."

"Hey, there's your sweetie now."

"Fuck, what's she doing with Palmer?" Jake frowned as they headed her way. "Andres." He called out.

"Hey Jake, Gabe." Catia smiled as she waited for them. "How's it going?"

"Good. Where you headed?"

"East side."

"With Palmer?"

"Yeah."

Jake snarled as he moved closer. "Be careful."

Her head tilted.

"Be on your toes with him, all right?"

"Yeah, sure. No worries, Jake."

Jake's gaze narrowed as she headed out the door. "I don't trust that guy."

"I know what you mean." Gabe said. "I think Carter's on the East side this morning too. Let's go have a talk with him and Bradley."

~~*~~

Jake laughed with Gabe as they headed up the stairs from the garage.

"I can't believe you still haven't figured it out yet." Gabe chuckled.

"Just spill."

"It's someone you know."

"No shit, dickhead."

Jake and Gabe turned when the desk Sergeant yelled for them. "Hey Sarg, what's up?"

"I need you two to run down to Mercy. We have an officer down, gunshot, friendly fire."

"There's no one else in the squad room?"

"Not right now, and Jake, you'll want this one."

Jake frowned as Matilda leaned forward.

"It's Andres."

His eyes went wide as he turned and ran for the stairs.

~~*~~

Jake yanked the curtain aside, his gaze found Catia as she sat on the gurney, arm lifted as the nurse bandaged her up. "Are you all right? What the hell happened?"

"Jake?"

"Yeah, Jake. What the hell happened, Catia?"

Her gaze narrowed with pain as the nurse tightened the dressing.

"Sir, if you can't calm down, you'll have to leave," the

nurse turned toward him. "Officer Andres, lie back, please. The doctor will be in shortly."

"Sorry," Gabe said as Jake moved over to the other side of the gurney. "Detective Mac Cloud, Special Investigations. She's a friend."

Jake noticed the nurse nod as he met Catia's gaze. "What happened? Sarg said we had an officer down, gunshot, friendly fire."

"Yeah, Palmer's a fucking idiot." Grimacing as she laid back against the pillow, Jake helped her and pushed another one in back of her to help. "Thanks, Jake."

"What did he do?"

"He saw a kid walking down the road, swerved the car, almost hit the kid, and jumped out, gun drawn. The kid was scared shitless, followed all commands and Palmer wanted to shoot him. He kept yelling at him for no reason. I told him to stand down. He refused. It was like he lost his ever-loving mind, Jake. I stepped in front of the kid when Palmer refused to listen to me, even after I called it in. He needs his damn badge and gun taken away."

"Where the hell did he shoot you?"

"My vest, mostly."

Jakes eyes widened. "Mostly?"

"Several shots grazed me. I jumped in front of the kid and took the hits."

"What the hell do you mean, you jumped in front?"

"The kid was still lying face down on the ground. Palmer would have shot him in the back."

"Fucking A, I'll kill him!"

"Jake, settle down," Gabe said. "If you can't, then step outside. We need to debrief her about the incident."

Jake met Gabe's gaze, nostrils flared, chest heaved.

When Catia set her hand on top of his, he breathed deeply, exhaling slowly. "I'm fine." Jake moved a bit to the side as Gabe questioned her and the more pissed he became. Palmer needed a hefty punch in the face, that guy was a ticking time bomb. They'd heard rumors of his actions, but no one who rode with him would open their mouths. Personally, he knew Palmer must have intimidated them in some way. Jake took his cell out as Gabe wrote down her answers. "This is Detective Jake Mac Cloud, badge four fifty-nine, SIU is investigating the incident of Officer Palmer discharging his weapon on Officer Andres. I want the body camera footage from both officers downloaded to my email now. Thanks, Gertie."

Jake turned when Gabe asked, "Did he say why he went after the kid?"

"No," Catia said. "I tried getting more out of him, trying to figure out what the hell was going on. It was like he was gunning for this kid." She looked up at Jake. "His eyes, I haven't seen that in a while."

"What do you mean?" Jake asked as he moved to sit on the side of the bed.

"You know when an officer sees too much violence, active shooter aftermath, war. They get this look in their eyes. He had that look, Jake. When he pulled the trigger, I could see it coming. It was like I was having an out-of-body experience. I could see everything happening in slow motion, his finger tightened on the trigger. I remember moving to cover the kid more effectively and hearing four shots. I felt the hit of them all as sirens sounded in the background. Two hit my vest, one my arm, and the other the bottom of my vest along my side. After the first hit, I jerked back, then started going down with the second. I lost consciousness when the fourth one grazed my side as I was hitting the ground."

Although Jake kept her gaze, he could tell she was re-living it by the glazed look in her eyes. When she stopped he ran his thumb over the top of her hand and watched as the glazing went away when she blinked.

"I knew I wasn't going to die, but I was so afraid he'd still go after the kid."

"From what I've heard, he's all right, shaken up, but okay."

"Yeah, I made the doctor tell me the minute I was conscious."

"Gabe."

"Yeah?"

"Turn away." Jake waited until he went out the door, before leaning in to kiss her softly, his thumb gently stroking her cheek. "My God, Cat. When I heard it was you down with a gunshot, I couldn't get here fast enough. Please tell me you're all right."

"I'm all right."

"You do know, you're on paid admin until I.A. clears you."

"Yeah."

Jake backed up when the door opened, and a doctor came in. "Can she go home?"

"Certainly, with a few directions. Will you be driving her, Detective?"

"Yes." Jake let Gabe know he'd be at the station as soon as he got her settled and helped her get her uniform shirt back on.

"Jake."

"Hmmm?" his fingers moved to another button.

"You're making getting dressed so sexy, I may need you to dress me every morning."

Jake smiled as he met her gaze. "Wait until I undress you."

~~*~~

Jake got her home and on the way into her apartment, George ran out to see them, his smile turning from happy to worried. "She's okay George, just a bit sore."

"Are you sure Jake? Ms. Catia, are you sure?"

"We're sure. She just got bumped up a bit." Jake smiled when he ran back home. "He's a good kid."

"He is, and you do well with him." Catia said.

"I like kids."

"Me too."

Jake wiggled his brows at her as he opened her door. "All right, Starsky. Let's get you to bed."

Catia chuckled. "Oh, damn, Jake. Don't make me laugh- it hurts."

Jake helped her sit on her bed slowly. He knew what it was like to get shot, both vest and flesh. Moving, he unhooked her gun belt and followed her instructions to hang it up on the back of her bedroom door. Turning his gaze, he followed her fingers as she started unbuttoning her uniform top. He liked how she wore a sports bra, instead of a regular one. Her breasts would fit nicely in his hands with a bit extra. He loved extra more for playing with. Jake stepped forward, brushed her fingers out of the way, and continued down the shirt. When he had it off, he ran his fingers along her bra. "Want this on or off?"

"On is fine. I don't feel like lifting my arms to get it off."

"I like how you wear the sports bra. It looks good on you."

"More support."

Jake noticed her quick breath when he ran his fingers along the sides of her breasts. "Sorry Cat, I don't mean to cause you pain."

"It's not pain, Jake. It's arousal."

"Shit, honey. I'm sorry. You're hurting and I'm all touchy-feely."

Catia smiled. "Don't be, and I like it when you call me Cat."

Jake rose up, smiling. "All right, let's get these pants off." He did it as quickly as he could, steeling himself as his hard cock pressed even more against his jeans. "Cat, I'm going to have to scoot for now. I'll be back later with something to eat. Ok, gotta go. Later, bye."

"Bye, Mac Cloud. Don't forget to grab my key hanging by the door so you can feed me later."

CHAPTER 4

CATIA TILTED HER HEAD AS she listened to Jake. He had been true to his word and brought back Italian food. "So, what you're saying is, Gabe doesn't like Mitch's wife because he thinks she stepped out on him before the wedding?"

"Yep. Mitch has defended Celia, telling Gabe it wasn't what he thought, but Gabe's seen her with some guy named, Thigpen."

Catia whipped her eyes to him. "Thigpen?"

"Yeah, Josh, John, James, something like that, anyway some douche from I.A."

"Celia works for I.A.?"

"Yep, she's a civilian, does secretarial, admin. Anyway, from what Mitch says, the guy, Thigpen, was making moves on her. Celia knew and some detectives at I.A. were always blocking him from her. From what Mitch says, the day Gabe saw her, Celia was running out of a hotel. She didn't know it was Thigpen there; she thought it was a buddy of ours, Nick, on a sting and needed paperwork. Thigpen attached her, I mean, bleeding, bruised the whole nine yards. Celia was able to hit Mitch's number during the attack," Jake chuckled as he bit off some garlic bread. "I thought Mitch was going to pound the guy into next week, it took Gabe and several Detectives at I.A. to hold him back."

"I hope she put in for a transfer."

"Oh, hell yeah. Mitch stormed I.A. like a damn tornado. But shit, Cat. I've never seen a man run so fast in my life as to see Thigpen running from Mitch."

Catia frowned "You were there?"

"Yeah, Zack was with him in briefing and called me after he called Nick. I got there as Gabe held him back. Some of the detectives over there who know us kept Mitch under control until Zack could get there."

"Was there a hearing on Thigpen?"

Jake snorted. "Yeah, he got a slap on the hand. He has a few friends higher up that got his ass out of trouble."

Catia's eyes narrowed. "A few friends higher up?"

"Some Captain and Lieutenant spoke up for him, and boom- it's like nothing happened. If you ask me, I.A. needs an I.A. to make sure they're following the same policies."

"I agree. You have good and bad in I.A. Jake, just like the rest of the force."

"I know. It just pisses me off with all this shit now a days and asses like Thigpen can still sexually harass a woman and get away with it."

"I hear ya." Sucking until her straw hit air. She placed the to-go cup on her end table. "Damn, that was good. Where did you stop?"

"A little place down off Vineland. But if you like seafood, I'll take you to Lei's once you're able."

"Oh, I love seafood."

Catia smiled when he placed a kiss on her cheek before gathering their trash up and heading to the kitchen.

"Jake."

"Hmmm?"

Catia glanced over at him as they watched tv from her

bed. "I have something to tell you, but, well, you're not going to be happy."

"What do you mean?"

Catia met his gaze. "Promise me you won't be mad."

"I can't promise that until you tell me what it is."

Her chest rose quickly. "Ok, that's fair. Just promise you won't yell."

"Okay."

"I like you Jake, but I have to get this off my chest."

"I like you too, honey." He turned onto his side. "And your chest."

"Damn, Jake." She smacked him lightly as he chuckled. "I'm trying to be serious here."

"Well go on then, spill."

Catia breathed out heavily through her nose. "I'm the bee." She said quickly, not sure if he heard her until his eyes widened and then he bust out laughing.

"What's so funny?"

"You, you're the bee. Christ, babe."

Catia frowned as he kept laughing. "I'm tired. You can leave now."

"Oh baby, I'm not going anywhere."

"Then you stop laughing at me. I'm serious here and you, you're laughing at me." Cat turned, giving him her back. When he stopped laughing, he shut the tv off. She could hear him taking his jeans off, and then he was under the covers. She liked his strong warmth on her back. He was close-spooning her, his head on her pillow.

"Bzzzz bzzzzz."

"You're so damn infuriating, Mac Cloud." Smacking his thigh, she left her hand there. Damn, she hadn't realized she was tired.

Jake

~~*~~

Catia smiled when he wrapped an arm around her waist. He was sexy as hell to wake up next to. Cuddling back up against his chest, she didn't want to move out of the warm cocoon. His warm breath on the back of her neck sent tingles coursing through her body, and she groaned when lips moved along her skin. Lips parted, his hand moved up between her breasts to her throat, holding her to him as he nibbled and sucked. "Oh damn, Jake." Her ass ground against him and rubbed his hard dick, eliciting a moan from him, a throaty male moan and he pushed back.

"Fuck baby, when we get it on, it's going to be rough."

"I like it rough…" she breathed. Both stopped still when a knock sounded on the door. "I'm not expecting anyone."

"Me neither."

Catia rolled as he jumped out of bed. Tossing his jeans and t-shirt on, he grabbed his gun on the way out. Sitting up a bit, she could hear him ask who it was and knew he was looking at them through the peep hole, then his harsh tone as he told someone to stay there.

Catia met his gaze when he entered her bedroom.

"It's I.A. They want to speak with you."

"Oh, here. That's weird."

"Right. That's what I said."

Catia frowned as he sat on the bed and put his socks and boots on. "Jake, who is it?"

"I don't know, two guys I haven't seen before, but their badges check out."

"Names?"

"Ah, Torres and Edwards."

Catia gaze narrowed. "Jake, can you help me get dressed?"

"Yeah honey, no worries."

Cat grimaced when she had to lift her arm.

"Don't you have a button up shirt?"

"No, just my flannel."

"Where is it?"

"Closet."

Catia walked slowly to the living room where Torres and Edwards waited. "Good morning, Detectives. How can I help you?"

"We're here to debrief you, Officer Andres," Torres stated.

"Special Investigations already debriefed me."

"So we can see."

Catia's brows arched. "Excuse me, detective." Her tone was pointed; it wasn't a question.

"Detective Mac Cloud, you can leave." Torres said.

"I don't think so." Jake stated as he stood by the side of the sofa, taking her arm to help her sit down.

"We do." Edwards said as he stepped forward. "We've read SIU's debrief, and we're here to take care of it on our end."

Catia eyes widened as a testosterone pissing match started between the three. Jake was not backing down. "All right! That's enough!"

Just then, Jake's cell went off and he looked at her with the "I have to go" look.

"I'm good, I'll have Georgie come over and help me out when he gets home. Wednesdays are half-days."

Jake nodded. "If you need me, call."

Catia nodded as he left, shutting the door behind him. No one spoke until his Harley started.

"So, Andres, does the boss know one of your targets is having sleepovers?" Torres asked.

Her gaze whipped to his. "Nothing happened, moron. I'm not that stupid," she growled. "The boss is aware of every aspect of this investigation. Jealousy doesn't become you Torres, and it doesn't work with me. So back the fuck off and straighten yourself up while you're in my house, you son of a bitch, or I'll take you down several notches and send you home crying to your mamma."

"Andres, can you give us the detail of what happened yesterday?" Edwards asked.

Catia tilted her head, brows lifted, and waited until Torres backed up to her breakfast bar before she looked at Edwards and debriefed. "I'm telling you, the one you need to get an investigation on is Palmer. That one is a loose cannon and a liability to the department."

"All right. Thanks, Catia. We'll report to Thigpen and get this in the system to get you back out as soon as you're released from medical."

Catia's gaze followed them out of her house. Her stomach turned from what she'd been sent in here to do: investigate SIU, especially the Mac Cloud brothers, to make sure they were following policy and departmental procedure. It wasn't a bad assignment; she could target anyone. What she didn't expect, was to fall for one of her targets. "Damn."

Thank goodness this case wasn't the main reason she had moved from Miami. If it was, she'd have a major issue on her hands.

Catia stayed on the sofa. She hadn't realized getting

shot would take so much out of her, but damn! And the bruises where the two hit her vest, she'd be sore for at least a week. Hopefully they didn't keep her on medical that long. Glancing over when the door clicked, her gaze went to where she kept her keys. They were gone, and Jake walked through with bags.

"Lunch is here."

"I was wondering who was coming through my door. I hadn't realized you took my keys when you left."

"Never gave them back." He smiled. "They were still in my pocket when I tossed my jeans on this morning. Found them when I undressed to take a shower."

"Oh, that's good."

"That I found them?"

"That you showered." She chuckled.

"Smart ass, I didn't know what you'd like, so I picked up some tempura fried fish and sushi from Lei's."

"Two of my faves."

"Good, and after we eat, I'll help you get into a hot bath. It will help with the soreness. I also picked up some bath salts and chamomile mint tea."

Catia grinned as she watched him take everything out of the bags. She'd never had a man so thoughtful as to bring her salts and tea because she was hurting. "Thanks Jake."

"You're welcome. How'd it go with those two dickheads?"

"Fine. They asked, I told, the usual debriefing when something happens."

"Yeah, but something was up with those guys. That Torres, I got bad vibes off him."

Her head lowered a bit as she continued to follow his

movements. Yeah, she did too. Jake looked like a damn rough rider, someone who would throw down in a minute and he probably would if he had to, but this side, this side of him was defiantly tearing down her walls. "You're tearing down my walls and I don't like it." She met his gaze and, surprise, stared back at her, before he smiled.

"I have mine too, honey, and you've already hit a few yourself."

Her brows lifted, eyes wide. "Me? I don't understand." His hands stopped moving, forearms resting on his thighs, hands hanging between his legs as he met her gaze.

"You with Georgie, you don't treat him differently than other children because of his disabilities. You tell it the way it is. If I'm an ass, you call me on it. You don't let it go because you like me, you eat, like a real person. Christ, I think I got a woody when you piled down that burger and sides last weekend, and you allow my family to invade your living space and start inviting others if they happen by."

"But that's just, I mean…"

"That's you and I like it."

Her eyes fluttered when his lips touched hers. Damn this man, she liked him too, just a little too much, her palm settled on his chest. The warmth radiated off him, and muscles twitching beneath her fingers had her pussy clenching.

"All right sweetheart. Eat now, kiss later. I'm starving."

"My God, you're such a man."

"That's a good thing."

Catia rolled her eyes at his grin. "Hey, how come you call me 'honey' when we're talking about something important and other pet names when we're not?" she asked as she lifted the fork with fish.

"Your hair reminds me of honey at nighttime with your highlights, like amber almost. I can't call you 'caramel', so 'honey' is the next best thing."

Her mouth dropped. "Caramel?" and then she busted out laughing, grabbing her side. "Holy shit, Mac Cloud. You're going to be my downfall."

"As long as you're falling in bed with me, I'm good."

"You're single-minded, Mac Cloud: food and sex."

"That's more than single, Andres. Didn't they teach you how to count in Miami?"

"You're cruising for a bruising, Jakob Mac Cloud."

~~*~~

The moment he left, and she heard his Harley pull out, she grabbed her cell phone and called her boss. John Thigpen, and filled him in on what she found out. "Sir, I'm just not seeing where SIU or the Mac Cloud's are breaking any policies or procedures. They go by the book. I've never seen the likes of it."

"That's bullshit, Andres. Are you sure it's not because Jake spent the night?"

Catia sat up. "Excuse me, Sir. Let me make this as perfectly clear to you as I did to Torres. I'm not that stupid. If you doubt my word, then you pull me right now. But I will not be accused of compromising my assignment. Do I make myself understood?" She was pissed. She couldn't stand the little bastard anyway.

"No, no. I'm not yanking you, stay on them! I want something, I don't care what it is. You bring me anything on the Mac Cloud's do you hear me! Sleep with him, sleep with all of them, you do your job and bring me something to bring them down!"

Jake

"I haven't found anything on them. They are clean."

"Then make something up, you hear me? I don't give a damn what you have to do, do it!"

Catia's gaze narrowed as he hung up. Yeah, definitely something going on here.

CHAPTER 5

CATIA SMILED AS JAKE OPENED the door for her. He had stopped by to get her after work, so they could grab a drink at the Fay and then go out to eat. "You don't have to baby me."

"If I was, you'd be in bed and I'd be delivering the beer to you."

"Oh my God, what am I doing to do with you?"

"I can think of several ideas and positions."

Catia chuckled as they walked in and the place started clapping. Her face heated. She looked back at Jake. "I don't understand."

"Someone finally had the balls to stand up against Palmer and not let him intimidate them."

Her eyes wide. "How did you find out he stopped by?"

Jake's gaze whipped down to hers. "What the hell do you mean, he stopped by?"

Catia glanced around as the bar quieted. They were all listening. Damn, why did she open her mouth? "Ah."

"Yeah, Andres," Mitch said as he stepped up. "When did Palmer stop by?"

"I think I need to sit."

"You sure will, right after you explain yourself." Jake said.

"Um." Catia ignored meeting his gaze as she leaned

against a pool table. "Last week, after I.A. left, he kinda showed up and pushed his way in the apartment." Glancing up, her eyes widened when the veins in Jake's neck stood out and his nostrils flared.

"Why didn't you call me?" His tone was low, his words pointed.

"Because I handled it."

"The bastard shot you four times the day before." He growled.

"Yes, and I handled it."

"Catia!"

"Jakob!" she met his gaze, not backing down. "I handled it. If I couldn't, I would have called for a body bag instead of I.A. to report it to Edwards." Catia heard Zack say his name softly.

"Fine, but I'm not happy."

"Fine. Me neither."

His head did a double-take as he frowned. "What the hell are you mad for?"

Catia raised her hand, pointing at him. "You, Mac Cloud, you. Just, don't you start on me." She left him, brows raised, when she stepped over to the back booth and sat down with Gabe, who was all smiles. "What are you smiling at, Gabriel?"

Gabe chuckled as he held his hands up. "Damn girl, nothing. It's all good."

"Thank you, Walt," she said softly when he set a bottle in front of her on the table.

"You're welcome, kiddo."

Catia glanced back at Jake who was speaking with Zack in low tones. "You getting over here, Mac Cloud, and having a drink with me, or taking me home?"

"I'm coming. Damn, sugar. You can be a bossy bit of goods." Jake smiled.

"I damn well can, so don't forget it." Softening her tone and giving him a soft smile, she scooted in "Will you sit by me and cuddle?"

Catia chuckled when Jake swooped into the booth and wrapped his arm around her shoulders, placing kisses all over her face. "My God, I created a monster. Cut it out, Mac Cloud, my beer's getting warm."

Jake leaned back, arm still across her shoulders as Walt dropped a bottle in front of him.

~~*~~

Catia turned her head on the pillow, meeting Jake's gaze. "Hey, I have a question for you."

"Sure."

"Will you call me Caramel when I'm dressed like an exotic dancer?" she grinned when he blinked slowly, then hooted and suddenly he was on top of her. "Damn Mac Cloud," she laughed. "What are you, a part-time Ninja?"

"No baby. I'm all Mac Cloud."

Catia met his playful kisses and met his gaze when he stopped. "What?"

"I'm not loving you until the doc clears you and you've been back to work for three days."

Catia frowned. "Three days, where's that come from?"

"Experience, you'll be sore and achy. In fact, I won't show up for three days. Well, longer if I get an assignment."

She liked how her body fit with his. He was lying on top of her, nestled between her thighs, his elbows on the bed and thumbs brushing the side of her face lightly. "Does that mean we can't play?"

"Sorry, honey. I'll stay the night, but I'm pretty sure the doctor will release you tomorrow, so you'll be reporting for duty."

"And I'll see you in three days."

"Three days."

~~*~~

Catia smiled as she met John in the lobby. She was partnered with Sydney's cousin today because his partner was on vacation. "Hey, John."

"Catia, how are you?"

"Good, and glad to be back on duty."

"I see Jake's made himself scarce."

Catia chuckled as they headed out to the cars. "Yeah, some stupid three-day thing."

"They have some odd rules in that family."

"I'd say more superstition than rules. Hey, isn't Zack's wife your cousin?" she asked as they rode out of the parking lot.

"Yes, although if you ask her, I'm no better than the dirt on her shoe."

"Why's that?"

"She's still pissed at me from the case when Zack targeted her to make sure she wasn't stealing from the D.A.'s office."

"Yeah, I heard about that case. Didn't they hook up during it?"

John snorted. "Right, a Mac Cloud compromising a case. No. Especially Lieutenant Zackary Mac Cloud. He waited until he cleared her and then they got all cuddly. If it's anyone, Zack keeps the rest of them in line. He's a stickler for following the book. Don't get me wrong, they all do, but he's like the enforcer for them. He will bring them to task if they even think of riding the line."

"But, she forgave Zack, because she married him and she's still mad at you?"

"Yep. I'm family, I should have known better."

"Wait a minute. Wasn't it her sister who was stealing and the one who stabbed her?"

"Yeah, Lori. She's a piece of work, and sitting in state for another ten."

"Do you get along with Zack?"

"Oh, hell yeah, he's a good guy, great cop. We butted heads over the case, I didn't want him to lead her on and hurt her."

"That's understandable. Being undercover is not easy, especially when you fall for the target."

"You ever been undercover, Catia?"

"Yeah, a time or two."

"Not me, I don't have it in me. I do just fine right here in my car on the streets."

Catia smiled. "Yeah, it's really not to my liking either." John was a knowledge of information she couldn't find in the computer or files. She'd been targeting the Mac Cloud's and everyone they knew in the department since before they knew of her, before she set foot inside the station house.

~~*~~

Her mind was swirling as she jumped in the shower. She did her job and she did it well. That was why her new boss had requested her transfer. Because that's what she did, and she was good at it. "Damn, I need a new job."

Catia grinned as she stepped out of the locker room. She'd

taken a quick shower but was ready to go home and take a bath. Jake was right, damn it. She was sore.

"How are you feeling, sweetheart?"

Catia turned to see Jake leaned back against the wall, arms crossed, relaxed. "Sore. Yes, you were right."

Jake smiled as he came off the wall. "A lady who can admit when I'm right- I may have to keep you, Andres. Do you have enough bath salts?"

"Yes, thank you. I stopped and picked more up after the doctor released me for duty."

"I'd love to take you home, but I'm heading out on a case."

"I thought you were going to say the three-day thing."

"That too, but there's no reason why I couldn't help you into the bath tub again, you know, for safety, so you don't fall."

Catia chuckled as he wiggled his eyebrows. "Oh my God, you are too much. Any idea how long you're going to be gone?"

"Few days, maybe the end of the week. Unless something big happens."

Catia stepped forward. "Be safe." Lifting up she kissed him quickly.

"You too." Kissing her back, they separated when the elevator dinged, and Mitch stepped out.

"Catia."

"Hey Mitch."

"You ready?"

"Yep." Jake answered.

Catia noticed Jake hung back until Mitch was a foot ahead of him, then he grabbed her. His mouth covered and took control. Catia set her hands on his waist. "Damn, Jake."

"I'll see you when I get back."

"You better." Her lids fluttered open, his smile her undoing. "Damn it, Mac Cloud, get out of here before he comes looking for you."

~~*~~

Hair flowing free with the wind, Catia crossed the street, removing her sunglasses before entering the building. Showing her credentials, she waited as it was inspected. "Thanks." Nodding her head when it was returned to her. Stepping away she headed over to the stairs, going to administration, smiling when she walked in and saw the person she was here for. "Hi, Celia Mac Cloud."

"Yes."

Catia showed her, her credentials. "I know you may not want to talk about this, but I need to ask how you know John Thigpen."

"I'm sorry, but I'm not allowed to discuss this topic."

Catia sighed as she tucked her billfold into her back pocket. "You did see my credentials, I'm not regular I.A., but I need to know if you think he would, how do I say this, retaliate against you or anyone associated with your husband."

"Why? What's he done?"

"Nothing, yet, but I need to know if he would."

"I wouldn't put it past him."

Catia noticed how her hand shook. "You're afraid of him."

"Listen, I…"

"I know and I'm sorry I had to ask, but I'm working a case," Catia glanced around to make sure they were still alone, tone lowered. "A special investigation and it's probably going to piss a lot of people off. I'm just trying to get my facts."

Celia met her gaze. "I thought that might be the case. I've seen you here, going to the Fourth floor. And no, I haven't said anything to Mitch. I recognized you at the cook out."

"I thought you did. Listen, I can't…"

"I know and don't worry; Mitch and I have an understanding when it comes to our jobs. He won't hear it from me. About Thigpen, I'm not allowed to talk about what happened to anyone without HR and my superior present. If you are who I think you are, you can pull the files. Also, go talk to Penny in HR."

Catia nodded, turned, and left. Hitting the elevator button, she made her way to the District building, where Thigpen and I.A.'s offices were. It wouldn't look strange, her going into HR, she could make any story up she wanted for going in and HR couldn't tell Thigpen or anyone why she was there. Walking through the HR door, her head turned when a lady behind a desk to the left raised her hand, motioning her over. "Penny?"

"Yes. Cece, let me know you were coming, don't take your badge out, she told me, mum's the word on this."

"I'm running an investigation; can you tell me how she knows John Thigpen."

"She used to be John's secretary. He wouldn't stop hitting on her, and I mean he was just downright nasty in his attempts toward her, especially when she started dating Mitchell,"

"Mitchell, Mitch Mac Cloud with SIU?"

"Yes, OMG, Thigpen blew a gasket. He tried everything he could to break them up, including having Mitchell

52

followed, and attacking Celia on a false errand, we even think he's the one who sent another detective to kill them."

Catia frowned. "Has any of this been documented?"

"Hell yeah, that's why Celia was moved to the executive building and away from Thigpen. That guy is nothing but a sleezy pervert."

"Do you know why he wasn't fired?"

"Two guys he knew higher up went to bat for him."

Catia turned when the door opened. "All right, thanks Penny. I'll get that 401k form in as fast as I can." Nodding her head, she turned on her heel and headed for the door. Thigpen wasn't only after Mitch, but all the Mac Cloud's. Damn. She knew her gut was right. Thigpen was using his position for personal reasons. She lifted her cell. "It's Andres. Your assumptions were correct."

"So, he is targeting the Mac Cloud's for personal reasons."

"Yes, sir."

"Your findings?"

"Once again, the Mac Cloud's are clean as is SIU. I can find no discoveries where they have veered away from policy or procedure on any of their cases."

"Stay on. I want to see how far Thigpen is willing to take this, and Andres, targets are clear, need to know only."

"Yes, sir." She was surprised he gave her the all clear to inform her targets of the investigation if it came down to it.

~~*~~

Catia grinned, the excitement built inside her all day. It was the end of the week, the end of Jake's self-imposed three-day rule and he was cleared by her heads, thank God.

Jake

She heard Jake was back in the squad room. Heading up from the locker room, she passed the desk, only to turn on her heel when the Sergeant called out to her. "Yes?"

"Jake's not up there. He just left on his bike, I think he was going to the Fay."

"Thanks, Sarg." Heading to the garage, she hopped on her bike, and started putting the helmet on. Stopping, she looked at it for a moment. She told him, it wasn't her fault he laughed at her. Strapping it onto the back, she headed out. Hitting the freeway, she gunned it. Catching up with Jake, she pulled alongside him, smiling when he turned his head. His eyes widened, and she blew him a kiss. Hitting the gas, she looked in her side mirror to see he'd straightened up and came up along the other side of her. Leaning down, she gunned it, heading for the Fay. She was sitting on her bike when he rolled up and parked it. "I told you it was my bike."

"And I told you it was going to be rough."

Tingles swam through her with his words, Kegel muscles clenching with want. She followed him as he grabbed her hand on the way into the bar.

"I thought I heard the bee." Zack said from the end of the bar.

"Yeah, do not disturb." Jake growled.

"I think you better put the music on." Catia said as she went by Zack.

"It's soundproof."

"What is?"

"The bedroom."

Catia kept up with his long strides. Lips parted a small eek slipping out when he shut the door the moment they stepped foot in the apartment, and her back was against it, his mouth on hers, hard, controlling.

Catia met him, tingles swarmed, muscles clenched, and she moaned when he lifted her, his cock hard against her pussy, jeans keeping them apart.

Jake grunted when *AC/DC's Thunderstruck* rang loud and clear from downstairs. "That smart ass."

"Huh?"

"Zack." Grabbing her shirt, he ripped it up and off. "No turning back, baby. If you want out, you better say so now."

Catia grabbed the hem of his shirt, lifting it over his head and tossing it when, "you've been thunderstruck" echoed out. Yanking his head toward her, she thrust her tongue into his mouth, and he followed, engaging back just as hard.

Clothes quickly were out of their way, his mouth on her neck, her breasts, her breathing erratic, chest rising rapidly, moans escaping and then he was in her. "Oh God!" her pussy tightened around him, so thick. "Oh God, Jake!"

He held her legs as he thrust into her, her back hitting the door, his mouth on her neck, sucking, biting.

Catia could hear the door creaking every time he thrust, but she didn't give a damn. "Oh, oh, holy shit!" her body tightened, tingles, his voice egging her on. Catia screamed as the wave crested and flowed, her body jerked, glutes tightening as her muscles tightened against him hard and then he was groaning, his hips twitched, delving deep inside her. His hand gripped the back of her head and then he growled, thrusting hard once, twice and held still, before several small thrusts.

Catia wrapped her arm around his shoulders as they stayed against the door, breathing heavy.

Jake chuckled against her neck when Marilyn Manson's "The Beautiful People", started. "That fucker."

"Ooh." Catia held on as he grabbed her ass and moved away from the door.

"You all right?"

"Recovering."

"Good, because I'm not done with you."

Her Kegels clenched, and he chuckled. She caught the sight of half of their clothing on the floor before he kicked the door to the bedroom closed. His tongue invaded her mouth, kissing her deeply as his hands caressed her body. Catia tilted her head, relaxing into him, giving him control. "Jake."

"Hmm?" His mouth leaving nips along its wake, while her hands moved to the back of his head.

"Did we even use a condom?"

He chuckled. "Yes." As he knelt on the bed.

Catia put her hands behind her as he backed up, to see a condom on his semi hardness and his jeans hanging on his hips. Her nipples tightened more. "Damn, you're sexy," she breathed as he disposed of his boots and jeans.

"Finish getting undressed, honey. Like I said, we're not done yet."

Catia glanced down to see she still had her jeans on one leg with her pink panties dangling. "Well, damn how did you do that?"

"Get up and do what I said, before I turn you over and spank that ass."

Her gaze whipped up. "Spank?" Her eyes widened a bit, then fluttered with lust and rolled over, giving him her naked ass.

"Oh, fuck yeah."

~~*~~

She didn't now how he did it, but Jake had managed to

make her knees weak and body sore from the passion they shared last night. Smiling, she poured a cup of coffee and grinned when lips appeared on her neck. "Good morning."

"It will be."

"Jake, oh." Before she knew it, he had her turned and half-sitting on the counter. Her pussy clenched and she nipped his bottom lip, moaning when he inserted a small butt plug into her ass. Her gaze was heavy with lust as she met his, her hips moving with the urge to sink her pussy onto his dick. Wrapping her leg around his waist, she moaned when he entered her. "When are you going to let me suck your cock?" she breathed as he thrust.

"When I'm ready." Grabbing her hip, he situated her better and then started thrusting.

Catia thought she saw the door open. "Oh fuck, yes." Tossing her head back, her eyes rolled as she saw a man's chest enter and then the door was closing, and she didn't give a damn which one walked in. All they could see were her naked legs and Jake's naked ass.

"Someone just walked in."

"Yeah."

"Do you like that?"

Catia met his gaze. "It was fucking hot, not knowing who saw."

Jake groaned, grabbed her by the back of the head and delved into her hard.

Catia cried out as his hard cock attacked her with no holds barred. The plug moved in her, ripples coursed through her. "Oh fuck, Jake."

"Cum for me."

Catia did and he held her secure as she toppled.

CHAPTER 6

CATIA GLANCED AT HER CLOCK as she went to open the door. "You're a little late, Mac Cloud."

"Sorry, honey." Jake said as he dropped a kiss on her lips. "I brought dinner."

"How'd it go today?"

"Better than average, you?"

Catia chuckled as she sat at her bistro table. "Fine, I'm with John until the end of the week."

"He's a good guy." He shoved a fry in his mouth as he set her dinner on the placemat for her. "Sydney's still pissed at him."

"Yeah, he said that."

"She'll get over it. Shit, she forgave Zack and married the ass. What shift are you working tomorrow?"

"Days for the rest of the week, then mids for two and nights."

"God, I hate that shift-switching shit."

"Ah, it's not bad once you get used to it."

"So, what do you want to be when you grow up, Andres?"

Catia laughed. "Really?"

"Yeah." He smiled back.

"I wouldn't mind being in a supervisory position, you know, out of the field but not out of the field."

"Really?"

"Yeah." She met his gaze. "I'd be on a regular schedule, although I'd probably be on nights to start, being the low man on the pole." She shrugged. "But then, I wouldn't have to be in the field as much."

"I live for the field."

"I know." She smiled. "But that's all right. I'll get you to eat healthier one of these days."

Jake chuckled. "I'm down for that."

"So, are you going to tell me what was up with the music at the Fay?"

Jake laughed. "You may not like it."

Catia's brow raised.

"They found out awhile back, and I'm talking high school, the first time I had sex was to those two songs. It was at a bonfire and that was playing on the radio."

"Ah, what?"

"Gabe and Zack were at the same party. They came looking for me and—"

"And?"

"I had her up against a tree." He shrugged.

Catia smiled. "I like getting it on to music." And she loved his dominating ways during sex.

~~*~~

Catia rubbed the towel over her hair as she stepped out of the shower. "Ooo."

"Shhhh." Jake whispered in her ear.

"Mac Cloud, what are you doing?"

"Sexing you up. I have to hit the road, honey."

Catia closed her eyes as he removed the towel wrapped around her torso. "How long?"

Jake

"Not sure." His mouth was on her neck.

Catia tilted her head to give him better access. "I don't think this is allowed, Jake."

"No one saw me, if you'd rather go to the truck…"

Catia turned in his arms, lifted up on her tiptoes and found his mouth with hers.

"It's gonna have to be quick."

"I know."

"I'll make it up to you."

Catia stepped more into the cove as he lowered his jeans, rolling a condom on. Her mouth watered with the need to suck his thick cock.

"Put your hands on the wall and thrust your ass out."

"Why don't you put my back against the wall, so I can feel you against me."

Jake stopped, lifted his gaze to hers, brow raised.

"Well, that's not very intimate and I want to feel you against me. You'll be gone for who knows how long." Damn, she knew he'd make her pay for questioning him and that made her pussy clench.

Jake grabbed her, lifted her back to the tile. "Hands up."

Catia lifted her hands above her head and he grabbed them in one of his, holding them to the tile wall as he thrust into her. "Ohhh."

"Shhh." His mouth claimed hers. "I want you quiet when you cum for me, do you understand?"

"Yes."

"No noises."

"Jake?" she whispered.

Jake stopped moving. Catia met his gaze, lowered hers and remained quiet. He would control how she received her pleasure and when, and she loved it. Her pussy clenched when he thrust hard and kept up the rhythm.

Biting her lip, she met his gaze, her breathing erratic and when he nodded, her lips parted, breath coming out as she orgasmed, her body jerking against his. Her heavy arms lowered and lay her hands on his shoulders as he kissed and bit her neck, her Kegels clenched, twitching around his hardness as he jerked, going deep into her. Reaching out, she caught his ear between her teeth and nipped.

He grunted softly, his arms wrapped around her as his mouth found hers. "God, honey. You're going to be my downfall."

"I know what you mean."

Catia glanced around the corner into the locker room and waved, letting Jake know the coast was clear. Heading to the door, she opened it, checking out the corridor. "All right, come on, hurry up."

Jake scooted out to the hallway just as someone walked by. He lifted his head in acknowledgement and turned smiling to Catia. "Told ya we'd be all right."

"We were lucky." Catia chuckled and met him for a quick kiss. "Be safe."

"You too, honey."

Catia shook her head as he headed down the hallway and started toward the garage in the other direction. That man was going to get her in trouble. She smiled as her gaze lowered to the left. She liked his trouble.

~~*~~

Catia glanced around as she headed into the meeting with her boss. She had given him her report the day after she'd been on the phone with him, clearing all of SIU and the Mac Cloud's. "Hey Mary."

"Hey Catia, he's waiting for you."

Catia nodded and headed to the door with Chief Sanders' name on it, knocked once and entered, meeting Chief Sanders' gaze.

"Andres, please come in. Commissioner Ward will be joining us today."

Catia held her hand out to the police commissioner. "Sir."

"Inspector."

Catia sat down in the opposite chair and faced Chief Sanders. "It's like I reported, sir. SIU is clear. Thigpen is out for revenge and has Torres and Edwards in his pocket. Thigpen wants to bring not only Mitchell Mac Cloud down, but his family and SIU, because he was in fact sexually harassing Mrs. Mac Cloud and was brought to task for it. When I said he told me to do what it takes to bring down the Mac Cloud's he meant it, he told me to break protocol and sleep with Jakob or all of them, and if need be, make something up, whatever it takes to bring them down. I'm sure you've listened to the recordings."

"John Thigpen, Torres and Edwards, misconduct is beyond reproach."

Catia sat back as they discussed the case and outcome.

"Where are you headed after this case, Inspector?" Commissioner Ward asked.

"I'm not sure, sir. Why?"

~~*~~

Catia sighed as she moved her sunglasses into place. She didn't mind mids, but nights were her worst. She was naturally a morning person, and going to bed with the sun in the sky was not her idea of a good night sleep. Jake had been gone over two weeks. She knew undercover was what it was, but she missed him. She'd seen Mitch in the hallways at the station, he told her Jake was safe and healthy. That helped, somewhat. But damn. She wanted to lay eyes on his hot bod.

Catia chuckled as she hit the gas on her bike and took off toward the station. Lay eyes on him, hell. She wanted to jump his bones.

~~*~~

Catia glanced over as she drove through her apartment complex, her gaze on the Harley Fat Boy parked in her spot. Her breathing became erratic, nipples tightened and pussy clenched as she all but ran up the sidewalk to her apartment and flung the door open.

She met Jake's gaze as she slammed the door shut and unbuckled her gun belt.

"I've missed you, honey."

"I've missed you too." Catia stepped toward him, pushed him back into a chair and straddled his lap, her mouth meeting his, hard. Her body trembled as her bottom touched his hard cock.

Jake became more aggressive. His hands moved up her sides. Moaning at his touch, she nibbled his lip, bit down, and sucked it into her mouth with his groan.

His mouth moved to her neck, leaving nips in his wake, her hands moved to his shoulders. "I don't know how you do it so fast, but you need to get a condom on." Moving off, she unbuttoned her trousers and almost ripped the buttons off her shirt, her gaze on a condom being rolled over his fat dick. Thrusting her pink panties down, she straddled him, plunging herself onto his thickness. They both gasped, stilling all movement and savoring the feel of each other.

He gripped her breast, teeth nipping her engorged nipple and her pussy clenched, tightening. Catia grabbed the back of his head, meeting his mouth and thrust her tongue in. Hips lifted, she plunged downward. Moaning, tingles stormed her. She pounded onto him with deep, possessive strokes.

Catia cried out, her entire body arched, insides convulsing as tingles warped her body, her muscles spasming around his thickness. "Oh God, oh God."

Jake grabbed her hips, thrusting up, faster, deeper, giving her what she wanted, what she needed. "Ah fuck, honey. Cum for me."

Catia gripped his shoulders as she delved over the edge, his cock pulsing and groaning with his release.

Catia flopped against him, his arms cradling her to him, their chests heaving. His lips brushed across the ridge of her temple.

"Let's go do this in bed."

Catia held on as he rose, his engorged dick moved deeper inside her, hitting several nerves. Her body twitched as he held her legs around his waist.

~~*~~

Catia frowned. Hanging up the phone, she headed to the desk Sergeant, then straight to SIU. Zack was there. "Zack, I need a favor." Handing him a paper, her fingers moved, feet shifted as he read it.

His head tilted, gaze lifted to hers. "How did you do this?"

"Don't ask. Can you pull this off- now?"

Zack smiled as he took his phone out. "We'll meet you there."

"Thanks, Zack." Catia took off for her squad car. If it's one thing she hated, it was a bully. Hightailing it to the elementary school, which housed grades K – 5, she parked in front of the class room she knew her target to be in. Waiting for the sound of a bike, she saw Mitch rolling to a stop right beside her car and opened the door, getting out.

"Hey, girl, Zack sent out an all call to meet here."

"Yeah, I'll debrief when the others show." She didn't have long to wait as Jake and Zack showed up and then Gabe. She knew the kids were at the windows. Hell, who wouldn't be with four Harley's and a police car sitting in front of your school? "I don't like bullies."

"What do you want us to do, hang them up by their toes, baby?" Jake chuckled.

"Jen called me this morning. Georgie has been getting bullied by this one boy, and it was pretty bad yesterday. Georgie was saying how he knows a cop and guys who ride Harley's who are all cops. And this boy, well, he pushed Georgie and according to Jen, the school hasn't done a damn thing about this and it's been going on for a while."

"How did you get this cleared by the Chief?" Zack asked.

"All in good time, Zack. So, we're here today as a show of support that bullying will not be tolerated. And we have a certain boy who is being called upon to help us on an investigation."

"Holy shit, I think I'm in love with you." Jake said.

"Me too. Later, Jake, I'm working here." She smiled back at him.

"I see Georgie," Mitch said. "Third window up and he's definitely excited."

"All right men, let's go get our boy." Catia led the way.

"He's riding with me," Jake said.

Catia listened as they started to argue, and Jake stuck to his guns. "OMG you guys are a bunch of kids. Yes, he's riding with Jake."

"That's just because you're sleeping with him," Gabe grumbled.

Catia turned as she held the door open. "Gabriel Mac Cloud that is not true, and he called dibs."

Catia headed straight for the office. "We are here for George Jenkins. His mother is waiting for your call."

"May I ask what this is all about?" A female asked.

Catia turned, plastering a smile on. She knew this to be the principal. "Yes, ma'am. All I'm at liberty to discuss is that Mr. Jenkins is assisting our Special Investigations department." She motioned to the guys, who removed their sunglasses, and came up with their billfolds and badges. My God, they were awesome. She couldn't have planned that if she'd tried. "With a bullying case they're working on."

The look on her face was priceless and Catia wished she had a camera. "As you know, the Chief of Police and the Police Commissioner are very concerned about this issue and have taken measures to assist in any way we can."

"Ah, ma'am, they have the mothers permission." The secretary said.

"We will call him down for..." the principal started.

"That will not be necessary, we will be escorting Mr. Jenkins out of class. Show us the way, please." Catia smirked, winking at Jake as they followed the woman out.

Catia let her knock on the door and enter first, excusing

the interruption, and then Catia walked right in. "Mr. George Jenkins."

"That's me!" George said from his seat, hand raised. "Hi, Cat."

"Hi, George. George, we need you to help on a case Special Investigations is working on. Can you help us out?"

"Hi Jake! Yes, I can. Did you call my mom? Is it okay with her? Does she know, Mitch, that's Mitch and Zack and Gabe. I told you guys I knew them, and they all ride Harleys."

Catia held back a smile as he grabbed his backpack and turned to the teacher. "Please forward all schoolwork home to his mother, he won't be back until Monday."

"You're riding with me, kid." Jake said.

"All right! I'm riding the Fat boy!" George said as he ran out.

Catia nodded her head and smiled as Jake laid a hand on his shoulder as they headed out.

"Officer." The teacher called out.

Catia turned and noticed Zack held off to the side waiting for her. "Ma'am."

"Thank you," she whispered as she approached, while her class ran to the windows. "We've been trying to get administration to do something."

Catia handed her a card. "Call me if you need to."

"Thank you."

~~*~~

"How in the hell did you manage this?" Jake asked as George sat in Kline's office going over a few cases with him on bullying, and getting George's input on how they should handle cases when they come up.

"I pulled a few strings." Catia smiled.

"From Miami?"

Catia chuckled. "No. After Jen called me last night, I got on the phone with the Assistant Chief of Police's secretary and let them know how the 'no tolerance on bullying' was not being seen to as they thought, told her what happened and received a call the next morning from the ACP, worked out this and the school is going to be receiving calls today on when the police department, counselors, etc. will be in to train the teachers and teach the children."

"And how do you know the ACP's secretary?"

Catia smiled. "I have lunch with her weekly after we hit the gym."

"My God, woman. I'm going to crush you and not let go."

Catia screeched when he lifted her up, placing kisses all over her face.

"Hey Jake. I don't think you should be kissing up on Cat at work. You're being loud and I'm working here," George said.

"You tell him, George."

Jake chuckled as he set her down "All right, all right. I'll vamoose so you can work. Sorry, George."

"Ok, Jake. And be safe out there!"

Catia smiled as he turned and headed back to his chair beside Kline. "OMG, I just want to hug him and squeeze him and call him *George*."

Jake hugged her. "I know, right? Oh crap," he whispered when George looked up at them. "Let's get out before we get busted."

"Right behind you, Sergeant."

~~*~~

Jake frowned. Doing a double take, he turned back around to make sure he was seeing what he thought. What in the hell was Catia doing walking out of the executive offices housing the police commissioner and a few others, when she should be home sleeping, getting ready for her next shift?

Lifting his cell, he hit her speed dial, his gaze narrowing when she looked to see who was calling and let it go to voicemail. "Hey, it's me. I know you have tomorrow off after your shift so you can switch to days. Stop by my apartment when you get off." Leaving his address, he hung up as she drove down the street on her bike. Waiting until she was out of eyesight, he moved his truck into traffic and followed her to the district offices where Internal Affairs was located. Grabbing his cell again as he parked the truck a few blocks away, his gaze followed her as she ran up the steps. "Hey Celia. What's hanging, sister?"

"Jake, What's up, meathead? I'm working." Celia said.

"Yeah. Hey, you were transferred down to the executive office building, right? Working for a few of I.A.'s heads?"

"Yes, why?"

"You wouldn't happen to know why Catia would be in there do you or who she might be seeing?" There was dead silence on the other end. "Cece, you there?"

"Yeah, I'm here Jake. Listen, I, need to go okay? bye."

"What the hell?" She'd hung up on him, CeCe had never hung up on him.

~~*~~

Jake glanced at the clock when the sound of her bike

drew closer and then shut off. He waited until she knocked at the door before going over to it. "Hey."

"Hey." Catia smiled as she stepped in.

"Have you eaten yet?"

"I grabbed something a few hours ago. Why, want to cook for me?"

Jake met her gaze when she turned standing in his living room. It wasn't much, but then again, he wasn't here all the time. "Maybe. I have something I need to ask you."

"Sure, what's up?"

"Why were you at the executive offices yesterday before you went on duty?"

Her brow furrowed a bit. "Why?"

"I'd like to know." His arms crossed.

"I ran in to say hi to a friend."

"Oh yeah, who's that?"

"Does it matter?"

Jake didn't miss the fact that her hands went to her hips. "Yeah, actually, it does."

"Jake, are you jealous? It wasn't a guy or anything…"

"I'm, not jealous. I want to know why you went to the executive offices." His tone lowered.

"I told you."

He snorted. "Really."

"What's going on?"

"So, you went to see a friend." At her slow nod, he moved his gaze from hers with a chuckle. "Had a friend to go meet at the district offices as well?"

"Were you following me?"

"Nope. Not until you ignored my call coming out of the exec building and went straight to I.A.'s, staying there before your shift started. So, tell me Catia. What the fuck is going on."

"Shit, Jake."

Jake eyes narrowed when she turned her back to him, paced a few times before she stopped to look at him.

"Don't even think to tell me it has to do with that idiot, Palmer."

Her lips thinned. "I can't."

"Why the hell not?"

"Don't you raise your voice to me, Mac Cloud."

"I'll raise my damn voice! You better come out straight with me Catia, if that's even your damn name."

"Of course it's my name. Damn Jake, stop it."

"Then tell me the truth!"

"I can't!"

"So, you've been fucking lying to me about something and won't come clean?"

"It's not that I don't want to Jake, I can't."

"Can't? Try *won't*."

"Jake, stop. Please, stop. It's need to know and you..."

"You come clean with me right now!"

"I'm I.A.!" she cried out.

CHAPTER 7

Jake stepped back, eyes wide as he stared at her. "I.A.?"

"Jake, I, I wanted to tell you, but I couldn't. I shouldn't have just now, but please understand, you know what it's like being undercover."

"At what, spying on my team or the station house?" When she didn't answer or meet his gaze, his widened as he stepped up to her. "Are you shitting me?" he growled.

"Jake, you know I can't talk about it," she whispered.

He drew back as if she'd struck him, brows lifted, and shook his head.

"Jake."

"Get out."

"It's not what you're thinking. Well, it is- damn, actually, it's worse, but…"

"Get. Out!"

"Jake, please…"

Jake sighed. "Just get out," he whispered. She nodded, her movements wooden as she turned and left his apartment. When she started her bike, he turned away, head lowered, and made his way to the bedroom.

~~*~~

"So, what's up? Celia said you called her at work the

other day and now Andres is nowhere to be seen." Mitch asked.

Jake looked up as his oldest brother sat before him at his desk. "What else did Celia have to say?"

"Not much. Said she couldn't talk about it, but she was worried about you."

Jake snorted. "Yeah, sure she was."

"Jake, what's going on, are you all right?"

"Oh yeah, fucking dandy." Rising up, he grabbed his bag and headed for the door. How the hell did he not see Catia was I.A.? How could he have been so stupid? He let her in, not only to his family, but she'd broken down several of his walls. He slammed his fist on the wall. "Damn it."

~~*~~

Jake steered clear of the guys all day yesterday; he just didn't want to talk to or be around anyone. They knew it and knew it had something to do with Catia as she was still missing in action. Lifting the beer to his lips, he glanced up when Zack greeted her and then the rest were saying hello.

"Ah. Hey, guys. I'm glad you're all here. I need to speak with you in private."

Jake snorted. "I bet you do, boss." Ignoring the looks from his brothers, they headed upstairs, heading over to the breakfast bar. He ignored them as they sat closer to the living room section, and took a swig.

"I, um, I have something I need to tell you all, and you're not going to be happy."

"No shit."

"Are you going to sit over there making shitty comments, Jake? Or are you going to join in on this?"

"Whatever you want boss."

"Well, I'm surmising by his attitude, he already knows." Gabe stated from the couch.

"Yes," Catia started. "We kind of, came to a head the other night."

"That's an understatement." Jake muttered.

Catia sighed. "I um, I'm not good at beating around the bush, so I'm just going to spit it out."

Jake glanced at her. Her chest heaved with a deep breath. She was nervous, and damn well. She should be.

"I'm I.A."

Jake turned his head. His brother's eyes went wide, Gabe sat up straighter, and Zack crossed his arms over his chest.

"I was sent in to investigate SIU, the station house, but especially, all of you."

"Fucking A." Mitch breathed.

"Yeah, isn't she just the dream." Jake said.

Catia met his gaze. "Shut the hell up, Jake. I had a job to do and I did it. You can't blame me for doing my job."

"Yeah," he snorted. "Did that include sleeping with me?"

Catia sighed. "You are such an idiot! I slept with you because I wanted to! Damn it Mac Cloud. Just- just- shut up and let me finish."

Jake swung his arm out, giving her cart blanche to do what she needed. She started pacing and he noticed how her jeans hugged every curve. The blazer she had on over a white shirt, her long hair swaying behind her hadn't gone unnoticed by him or his hard cock.

"Ok, I'm going to toss a name out there. John Thigpen."

Mitch came up. "What?"

"He's my boss, the one I report to and the one who sent me in to investigate SIU."

"Son of a bitch!"

Catia held up her finger. "Well, he thought he was my boss." She glanced-over at Jake and met his gaze. "You stated, you wanted to know why I.A. didn't have an I.A. watching their asses after Torres and Edwards came to debrief me."

"Yeah."

"I'm that investigational unit, Jake. I was called in to investigate Thigpen, Torres and Edwards, along with a few others. Especially when he made it known he wanted to send I.A. in after not only Mitch, but SIU and his family. I've actually been on this case since before Mitch and Celia started dating. Nick almost introduced Mitch to me once at district, but I ducked around the corner."

Jake turned a bit to meet her gaze more clearly.

"I'm new to the area, so I had to do my own investigations on why Thigpen would want to go after not only Mitch, but the rest of his family and SIU."

Gabe snorted. "Yeah, we all know why."

Catia turned from Jake. "Gabriel Mac Cloud, I'm setting you straight right now. I have been able to obtain and go through everything. I know what you saw, what you were made to see. Oh yes. You, my friend, were set up to see just what you did, and to act like you have been. Thigpen set the whole thing up. Celia has never, and I will beat you down if you still treat her like dirt after. But I say this with truth. Celia has never, messed around on Mitch, especially with Thigpen."

Jake met her gaze when she turned back to him.

"When you saw me, the other day coming out of the executive offices. I was leaving a meeting with the police commissioner and my boss Chief Sanders. I work in a joint task force for this specific reason. When Internal Affair officers use their positions for self-gain or satisfaction. We had come to a decision on how to proceed with the case. At first, they wanted me to stay in even after I cleared all of you, SIU, and the station house. Well, except for Palmer. That guy is just a loose cannon."

"Thigpen is going to be removed from duty along with Torres and Edwards." Her chest rose with a deep breath. "I'm sorry this happened to you guys, but I'm not sorry I'm the one they called in. I'm glad the uppers could see something was going on so one of Thigpen's flunkies didn't undermine the investigation. You guys do your job and you do it well. I'll be speaking with Captain Kline tomorrow to fill him on the details of the investigation, but as of a week ago, the case is officially closed."

"Geez, thanks," Jake snapped as she stuck her hands in her pockets.

"What do you want from me, Jake? Every single one of you know what it's like to be in my shoes. You've all been there. Just because I'm I.A. doesn't mean I'm out to get someone who's innocent. I do what you do, just in a different department."

"Sure, keep saying it; you may start believing it." He kept her gaze as she shook her head, turned for the door and left.

"Damn, Jake." Zack said.

"Yeah, man. That was a little harsh," Mitch said.

"Whatever. I'm out." Jake rose and headed out. He didn't need to hear their shit. They weren't the ones she lied to and slept with. "Wonder if she cleared me first." Hitting the gas, he took off.

~~*~~

Catia sat up glancing at the clock and sighed. Tossing the comforter, she hopped out of bed, and headed for the shower. She'd done nothing but toss and turn since she went to bed. She'd told Jake and his brothers everything she could about the case, she thought maybe just a little, Jake would understand. After all, he did this every day and he knew, coming clean to targets was something that was not done. She knew she was given clearance to divulge the case to them, due to their work and upstanding records. Blowing out a breath, Catia leaned into the hot stream of water. She couldn't even put herself in his shoes. Being targeted and falling for who did the targeting. Christ, she didn't know where to being with Jake, to try and fix this. All she knew, was she was miserable without him.

The station was quiet this time of morning. Heading up to SIU, she waited until Kline came in off the elevator.

"So, is it Detective or Investigator?"

"Investigator." Catia answered.

"They called last night after you left, filled me in on some of it. Come on in."

Catia nodded and stepped into his office when he opened the door.

"So, did you clear him before you guys hooked up?"

"Yes."

Kline nodded. "Thought so."

"You have a good team, Captain, and I'm sorry I set it on its ass."

"I've done my homework. You're good at what you do, Catia. Don't ever be sorry for that. This case just got a little harder because you and Jake started falling for each other."

"Yeah, well. The ending result still sucks."

"Sometimes it does."

Catia sat with him for the next two hours, going over the case and her findings.

"Well, I think that's it."

"You're a good investigator, Andres. If you ever want a job…"

Catia chuckled. "I think I blew that option out of the water, Captain. But thanks for the offer."

"Ah, Jake would get used to it. He'd just have to pull his pants up like a big boy."

Catia smiled sadly. "Somehow I don't think it would be that easy."

Kline sighed. "Probably right. But when I tell you that you have a friend with us here in SIU I mean it, Catia."

"Same here, Captain." She shook his hand. Her gaze settled on Jake and Mitch as they stepped to the door and he opened it for her. "Thank you, Captain."

"You remember what I said, Lieutenant."

Catia nodded her head in acknowledgement and stepped out, feeling the eyes of the detectives in the unit on her and stepped over to Mitch and Jake. "Hey Mitch, Jake." Her heart thudded against her rib cage.

"Catia." Mitch said.

Catia met his smile, her gaze going to Jake's back. "You're not mad at Celia, are you?"

"Nah, Cece and I have a code word for cases we can't talk about with each other, knowing it's business and not that we don't want to tell each other, it's just that we can't."

"Oh, that's good," her gaze went to Jake's back. "Jake, I won't say I'm sorry for doing my job, but I am sorry I hurt you." She knew he heard her although her tone was soft. Her chest ached as he strode off without recognizing her.

She blinked rapidly to stop the tears. "Well, ah… I'll catch you later, Mitch."

Mitch sighed. "Give him time, Catia. He doesn't understand right now that what you did actually helped. Thigpen was after all of us, because of me."

"It wasn't you, Mitch…"

"It was, and because he's a psychotic with a stalker mentality, he tried to hurt not only my family, but everyone in SIU and the station. You're a good investigator, Catia. Jake will come around."

Catia nodded. "Thanks, Mitch." Catia headed down to her locker, eyes on her every place she went. Word spread fast. Heading out she cringed when the desk sergeant called her name. Turning she met her gaze. "Yes, Sarg?"

"You're one of the good ones, Andres. Don't forget that."

Catia nodded. "Thanks, Sarg."

~~*~~

Four days later, Catia walked back into the station house. Heading straight to SIU, she was in her normal every day work wear. A pair of black slacks, form-fitting collared button down shirt, and a pair of heeled boots with her badge sitting on her left side right above her pelvic bone. Her hair hung loose around her shoulders, gun sitting on her right. Stepping into SIU Catia spotted her target and headed straight to him, and of course Jake had to be standing right there. He refused to call her back, so she gave up trying and it broke her heart.

Clearing her throat, she met Jake's gaze before turning to Mitch and Gabe. "Mitchell Mac Cloud, I need you to come with me."

"Catia?" Mitch asked, brow arched.

"What the hell do you want now?" Jake snapped.

"This is not your business Jake, but hey, thanks for talking to me. Mitch." She nodded to the door and left Mitch to follow behind.

When they stood in the elevator, she let out the breath she'd been holding. "Boy, he really hates me, huh?"

"I wouldn't say hate…"

"I would," she whispered, lowering her sunglasses as they stepped out to her car waiting.

"Damn, is this what you get to drive around in?"

Catia chuckled. "No, it's my personal car."

"Damn, Catia."

Catia sat behind the wheel of her 1968 blue Mustang. "This is my baby, and I thought you'd like to ride in it today rather than the Crown Vic."

"Hot damn, yeah. So tell me what this all about."

Catia smiled at him as she started the car up. "Trust me, you'll love every minute of it."

They drove for about fifteen minutes before she pulled up in front of the district offices. "Oh, by the way, I have Celia training here today. I thought she'd like a firsthand seat to the action."

"Are you going to spill?"

"You're my muscle."

"Muscle?" Shutting the door, he waited until she came around the front.

"To arrest Thigpen, Torres and Edwards." She grinned.

"Ho shit, Catia. You're not kidding, are you?"

"Oh, hell no. And yes, it's been cleared."

Catia smiled at Celia when they stepped into the building. The look she gave Mitch was priceless.

"I can't tell you, but stay there. We'll be right back," Mitch said on his way by his wife.

Catia headed up to Thigpen's office, nodding to the three uniforms there to meet her. She opened the door. The detectives present turned to see what was going on.

"What the fuck is this shit, Andres?" Thigpen yelled from his office.

Catia lifted her sunglasses to the top of her head. "Johnathon Thigpen, Jim Torres, and Paul Edwards, you are all hereby placed under arrest for the misuse and improper conduct of your positions within the Internal Affairs department. To name a few, harassment, intimidation, falsifying official documentation, misleading an ongoing investigation. Oh, and did I mention: it's Investigative Lieutenant, Catia Andres. Officers."

Catia stepped back as the three officers came forward, reading each of them their rights as they handcuffed them. Stepping behind them, she smiled as Celia ran up to Mitch when they entered the lobby. She gave them a few moments and stepped away. Stopping, she waited outside the doors. This case- this case had done her in mentally and physically. She was so done, being in the field, undercover. It's just not what she wanted anymore.

"So, what's your next assignment?" Mitch asked as they rode to the station.

"I don't know."

"Do you want to stay here?"

Catia shrugged. "I did."

"Catia, give him a chance to come around. He's stubborn like the rest of us and he's hurting."

"I didn't want to do that."

"I know, we all know, but sometimes it happens on a

case. Trust me, Zack never thought he'd go through it. Out of all of us, he's the by-the-book pain in the ass, and he fell hard for Syd. When there's chemistry, you have to go with it."

"I know. The last thing I wanted to do was hurt him, Mitch. I just…" Tingles swarmed her nose as tears entered her eyes. Pinching her nose with her thumb and forefinger she glanced over at him.

"You're hurting too."

"I don't know what to do." She whispered. "He won't call me, and earlier was the first time he's acknowledged my existence since he found out." Parking in front of the station, she turned to look at him.

Mitch patted her leg. "It will work out. Just hang in there."

CHAPTER 8

CATIA TILTED HER HEAD WHEN she heard a male asking for her. The low tone of his voice had her pussy clenching. Jake. Looking up from her desk, she saw her secretary escorting Jake to her office, and the look on her face was priceless. Her brows lifted as their gazes met. Catia stood up as they entered.

"Lieutenant Andres, Sergeant Mac Cloud to see you."

"Thanks, Jane," Catia waited until she shut the door behind her, before meeting Jake's gaze. "Hi, Jake."

"I went by your apartment, but George said you moved out."

"Yeah, that was for the case."

"Figured."

Catia nodded, not knowing what else to do. She hadn't expected him to walk right into her office. It had been two months, after all.

"Kept in touch with him, though. I mean, that's what he said."

"I have."

"That's good, he's a good kid. See you've moved up, huh."

"Yeah."

Jake nodded, thumbs hooked through his belt loops. "You in charge now?"

"Of this department."

"Huh. The case help you with that?"

"No, they wanted me to be the lead inspector in the field for the joint task force. I didn't want to."

"Why not?" His gaze finally met hers.

"I don't want to be in the field anymore. You Mac Cloud's were enough for me, I was sliced with a knife and shot four times UC."

"Huh, really? Sorry 'bout that. Well you didn't do too bad, Investigative Lieutenant sitting in the exec building."

Catia sighed. "Jake why are you here? We both know it's not for small talk."

"I wanted to see you."

"Oh."

"You hit me with a wrench. If it was anything I was not expecting you to say, it was that you were I.A."

"I know. I'm sorry Jake, I…"

"No, Catia, I'm sorry. I was so pissed, I thought you betrayed us, me. Damn, honey."

Catia stepped up to him and Jake yanked her into his arms. She melted against him, he buried his face in the crook of her neck.

"I'm sorry I was an ass. If you want, I'd like to see if we can do us."

Catia smiled. "I'd like that." Closing her eyes, she wrapped her arms around his waist.

"God, honey. I've missed you so much."

"I've missed you too. Damn, Jake." Catia moved her head, placing a kiss on the side of his neck. "How are we going to do this?"

"We just have a code word or something, like Mitch and Celia, goose liver, I don't know, so we know we can't talk about a certain case because it's..."

"Goose liver? Oh my God, Mac Cloud." Catia backed up, smacking him on the chest. "Seriously?"

"Yeah."

"But what about- what happened?" Catia twirled the hem of his t-shirt with her fingers.

"We need to talk about it, get it out so it's not sitting in the dark waiting to pop out. We'll figure it out."

Catia hugged him to her, loving the strong feel of him next to her.

"Are we allowed to kiss in here?"

Catia chuckled. "While it's not professional, it's not against regs." Lifting her head, she met his mouth, his lips soft yet dominant.

"Unlike what we did in the women's showers?"

Catia chuckled. "Again, not professional, and not in the regs, so shhh…"

The End

Want to know how it all started, how Mitch met Celia… Keep a look out for MITCH, coming 01.19.19.

Read Lots and Stay Spicy

C ~

Indulge in the Spicy Side of Romance

www.authorcasalo.com